T0265952

Michael Spencer

We Know Now
Snowmen Exist

Salamander Street

PLAYS

First published in 2021 by Salamander Street Ltd.
(info@salamanderstreet.com)

ISBN: 9781914228049

Printed and bound in Great Britain

10 9 8 7 6 5 4 3 2 1

THE DYATLOV PASS INCIDENT

In early 1959 nine Russian hikers went missing during a camping expedition in the northern Ural Mountains. Their tent was found to have been cut open from the inside and their belongings left behind. When the bodies of the group were later discovered seemingly having fled up to two kilometres away from the tent, five were found in a state of undress, while four were wearing pieces of their fellow hikers' clothing. Six of the expedition were deemed to have died from hypothermia, while three suffered fatal internal injuries including a fractured skull and major chest fractures. Unusually there were no signs of external injury, with the exception of one body which was missing its eyes and tongue.

An investigation by Soviet authorities at the time concluded that 'compelling natural force' had been responsible for the deaths, failing to account for several key questions: Why had the tent been cut open from the inside out? Why had the experienced group left their vital belongings behind? Why were some of the expedition found in a state of undress, while others were wearing fellow hikers' clothing? Why was one item of clothing found to be radioactive? How did three of the expedition suffer fatal internal injuries without any sign of external trauma? And why, according to some sources, did the final entry in one of the hiker's journals include the foreboding line *"...we know now snowmen exist."*

Over the years various theories – some significantly more outlandish than others – have been put forward to explain the circumstances surrounding the deaths. Some of the most prevalent include; an avalanche, katabatic wind, Yeti attack, infrasound induced panic, military testing, an altercation with local tribesmen, and even 'an internal group dispute leading to violence.' However no single theory appears to satisfactorily account for the variables.

Russian authorities opened a new investigation into the incident in 2019. On 11th July 2020 an avalanche was announced as the official cause of the nine deaths.

INTRODUCTION

Why was the tent cut open from the inside? Of all the questions posed by the tragic events of the northern Ural Mountains in 1959, this was the one which gave me chills. (Pun unforgivably intended.)

Having spent time immersing myself in the various mysteries surrounding the Dyatlov Pass Incident, I knew that I wasn't going to be the one to solve it. Nor to be fair, did I have the slightest interest in doing so. Mysteries so old they've passed into urban legend territory have no business being 'solved' anyway. Frankly, it spoils the fun.

But the concept of a small isolated group huddled together against the freezing elements, their tragic fate already decided — that felt like ripe territory for exploration.

Switching the events from late 50's Russia to modern Scotland and cutting the group numbers from nine to five (cue song) meant I could place the focus squarely on the individuals involved rather than allowing myself to get wrapped up in exciting but irrelevant Cold War era paranoia — even if a little dated spy-craft may have survived.

For those interested, my own personal theory as to what really happened to the Dyatlov Nine is buried between the lines of the text. But it's entirely incidental. This is the story of five friends laughing, peeing, and surviving together against the elements. But who, one day, on the side of a freezing mountain, make the choice to cut open their tent from the inside out.

Because they *Know Now Snowmen Exist*.

Michael Spencer, December 2020

CHARACTERS

CHLOE

HAYLEY

LISA

RACHEL

ZOE

We Know Now Snowmen Exist was first performed at The Old Fire Station, Carlisle on 29th August 2018. It subsequently transferred to The Space, London on 19th March 2019.

The cast *(in order of speaking)* was as follows:

CHLOE	Vanessa Sedgwick
LISA	Rowan Kikke
RACHEL	Rebekah Holly Neilson
ZOE	Naomi Webster
HAYLEY	Chloe Sturrock

Director	Lexie Ward
Lighting Designer	Andy Ball
Stage Manager	Kate Matthews
Sound Design	Lexie Ward
Produced by	Highly Suspect Theatre

We Know Now Snowmen Exist was supported by Elektronika, Carlisle Green Room Club, and Stanwix Theatre. Development workshops/ Originally produced by Adam Morley Theatre Company.

With special thanks to Hannah Allen, Alice Woodsworth, Rebekah Arthur, Lottie Hunt, Sinead Davies, Lesley Hayes, Dr James Issitt, Helena Brassington and Rebecca Gadsby.

ACT ONE

A tent seemingly in the middle of nowhere, set against a desolate snow-covered landscape. Harsh and unforgiving. A constant howling, bitter wind. Five figures emerge, dressed as though embarking on an Arctic expedition. They look to each other.

CHLOE: You realise there's only one thing left to do?

Everyone nods, solemnly.

CHLOE: Snowman?

EVERYONE: Snowman!

*In a blaze of excitement, hilarity and silliness, they begin to construct a snowman outside their tent. After a few moments, **LISA** pulls out her phone.*

LISA: Hang on, I know what this needs…

After a few swipes, music starts playing. It begins quietly, barely audible over the wind, though the girls can all hear it and are soon singing along. The music grows in volume almost drowning out the wind. They are in their element; singing, dancing and building their snowman.

Over this: The wind morphs into a static crackle. Overlapping bursts of news, media footage and soundbites from a variety of sources fade in and out.

ANNOUNCER(S) : …25th January 2018 a group of students set out into the Yapstovals mountain range…

…Charity expedition following the loss of fellow student…

…Eleven day trip to the summit due to be completed by 5th February…

…Confirmed by radio transmission…

…No signal received…

…9th February, Search and Rescue launched operation assisted by Mountain Rescue and helicopter scrambled from RAF Castletown…

…Hampered by snowstorms, search proved unsuccessful…

…No sightings at last known GPS location…

…Search continued bolstered with support from teams of dozens of volunteers.

…No sightings…

…Continuing the search…

…End of February, authorities declared the woman to be 'Missing, presumed dead.'…

…Search continues…

…Still no sign of the missing students…

…Charity expedition vanishes without trace…

…After one hundred and twenty-seven days of searching, bodies have been located…

…Lisa Cochran…

…Rachel Abbott…

…Bodies identified…

…Hayley Astley…

…Tragedy strikes as students…

…Chloe Beattie…

…Zoe Willis…

…Loss has greatly affected us all…

…Missing bodies found…

…Damaged tent abandoned within the Tokhal Pass region…

…Cut open from inside out…

…Bodies found wearing minimal clothing…

…Branches of nearby trees were broken, suggesting the women had attempted to climb…

…Cause of death; hypothermia…

…Wearing misplaced items of clothing belonging to their fellow campmates…

…Cause of death; hypothermia…

…Suffered fatal chest fractures, no other signs of external injuries…

…One body discovered missing tongue, her eyes and lips. Investigators believe injuries are unrelated to the cause of death…

…Families have been informed…

…*Cause of injuries unknown*…

…Tragic events…

…Inexplicable…

…Not the time for speculation…

…What happened to the expedition…

…Cause of death unknown…

…Accidental…

…Unforeseen…

…Horrific injuries…

…Tent cut from inside out…

…Missing tongue, eyes and lips…

…No external injuries…

…Cause of death hypothermia…

…Expedition member's journal found among the possessions…

…Final entry: 'We know now that Snowmen exist'…

The static between the various clips morphs back into the howling wind.

The Snowman is complete.

RACHEL: Can we get back inside now, it's fucking freezing!

They return to the tent. Only the Snowman and the wind remains. Or is it static?

Blackout.

INSIDE THE TENT

Sleeping bags, clothes, and all manner of random camping and hiking detritus litter the floor. Outside the howling gale continues.

CHLOE, **HAYLEY**, **ZOE** and **LISA** *are sat idly killing time.*

LISA: Eye spy…

ZOE: No.

LISA: …With my little eye…

HAYLEY: Fuck off.

LISA: …Something beginning with…

HAYLEY: Doesn't matter what it begins with.

LISA: *(Slowly.)* Beginning…

ZOE: Not this.

LISA: …With…

ZOE: Anything but this.

LISA: …With…

HAYLEY: Whose benefit is this for?

LISA: …With…

CHLOE: …With what?

LISA: And there's your answer.

HAYLEY: You just had to, didn't you?

She throws whatever is nearest to hand across the tent at **CHLOE**.

ZOE: Careful.

CHLOE: It passes the time! What else is there to do?

HAYLEY: We could gouge out our eyes? That might be more fun?

LISA: Unnecessary!

ZOE: Dark.

CHLOE: Enough suspense already. Something beginning with what?

HAYLEY: Kill me now.

LISA: Something. Beginning with. S.

HAYLEY: Sadist?

LISA: I knew you'd join in!

CHLOE: Sleeping bag.

LISA: That would be S B.

ZOE: Sleeping bag is two words.

CHLOE: It's one word.

LISA: No, it's two.

CHLOE: Are you sure?

HAYLEY: Go on a charity expedition to the arse end of nowhere, they said. It'll be fun, they said.

LISA: Definitely two words.

HAYLEY: You can leave all your troubles behind, they said. A chance to clear your head, they said.

ZOE: Who's 'they'?

CHLOE: Sleepingbag. It's just one word. Listen; Sleepingbag!

HAYLEY: You'll be with friends, it'll do you good to get away!

LISA: Saying it quicker doesn't make it true. It's two words. The word sleeping and the word bag.

HAYLEY: Kill. Me. Now.

ZOE: Inappropriate.

CHLOE: That's no argument. You could say that about anything. Horseradish is two words put together to make a bigger one.

LISA: Yeah but that's a horseradish. We're talking about a sleeping bag.

ZOE/CHLOE: Sleepingbag!

HAYLEY: It's not fucking sleepingbag! *(Pause.)* What the hell actually is a horseradish anyway?

CHLOE: It's a genius example of one word made up of two smaller ones…

HAYLEY: Not the word, the actual thing.

LISA: It's usually a sauce isn't it?

HAYLEY: But it can't just be a sauce, sauce isn't a natural state of being. You don't get animal, vegetable, mineral, sauce. It must be a thing before that thing is made into sauce. So what's the thing?

CHLOE: That's a surprisingly philosophical question for someone who didn't want to play eye-spy.

LISA: It must look something like a radish, probably.

HAYLEY: Why must it?

LISA: It's got the word radish in it.

CHLOE: So what? A dandelion isn't a big camp cat.

LISA: Shut up. I'm right. It's a vegetable that looks like something you'd find hanging under a horse.

HAYLEY: Sounds like your ex.

LISA: Vegetable, maybe. Hung like a horse, he fucking wishes!

ZOE: Wow. A new record. That was nearly ten whole minutes without mentioning a penis.

CHLOE: Poor Dave.

LISA: Don't start the 'poor Dave' shit, you have no idea.

HAYLEY: Dave-Ja-Vu?

LISA: Dave-Ja-Vu!

HAYLEY and LISA find this hysterical. CHLOE and ZOE exchange a look. This is an in-joke they're not part of.

ZOE: Dave-Ja-Vu?

LISA: He was a nice guy, a really nice guy.

HAYLEY: Fit too.

LISA: You think so?

HAYLEY: By your standards.

LISA: Cheeky bitch.

CHLOE: Is this the same Dave as Drama-Dave?

HAYLEY: No, Drama-Dave was one of Zoe's…

ZOE: He was not!

CHLOE: No, Zoe's was Drama-Tom. Long hair, cute smile, voice like a foghorn.

ZOE: Don't remind me.

CHLOE: He played Lady whats-her-name in *The Importance of Being Earnest*.

ZOE: Yep.

LISA: Yeah, he did. He was shit.

ZOE: I know.

CHLOE: I nearly wet myself when he said the handbag line.

HAYLEY: Why?

CHLOE: Cos I swear he said 'Ham-Bag'.

LISA: He did.

LISA/CHLOE: *(Impersonating him.)* '…A HAMBAG?!'

ZOE: Okay. Back to mocking your ex please.

CHLOE: You were saying about Drama-Dave?

LISA: My Dave didn't do drama.

HAYLEY: Dave-Ja-Vu studied, what was it, something about eight syllables long?

LISA: Biomolecular science.

ZOE: *(Counting this out on her fingers.)* Christ, that was a good guess.

HAYLEY: Biomolecular science, that was it.

LISA: Whatever the hell that is.

HAYLEY: The study of really small things.

LISA: Yeah, him and me both.

CHLOE: Why 'Dave-Ja-Vu'?

HAYLEY: Self-explanatory.

CHLOE: It's not self-explanatory or I wouldn't be asking.

LISA: He needed telling everything twice.

HAYLEY: *(Impersonating him.)* What was that, Leese?

LISA: That you need telling everything twice.

HAYLEY: *(Impersonating him.)* No, I don't.

LISA: Yeah you do.

HAYLEY: *(Impersonating him.)* What?

LISA: Yeah, you do.

CHLOE: Was he deaf?

LISA: What?

CHLOE: Was he deaf? …Oh. Well done.

LISA: No, just always distracted.

CHLOE: Mind on higher things?

LISA: So he said.

HAYLEY: It's never higher things it's other things.

LISA: Give him some credit, he worked hard. Whatever it was he actually did.

HAYLEY: Or worse, other people.

LISA: He liked the nickname.

CHLOE: Dave-Ja-Vu?

LISA: He thought it meant cos once was never enough.

HAYLEY: But you never find that one out until it's too late.

LISA: What?

CHLOE: More like Dave than you think.

LISA: What's up.

HAYLEY: Nothing. Forget it.

CHLOE: You okay?

LISA: It's fine.

CHLOE: Okay.

Something is not being said. It hangs heavily in the air. Eventually **ZOE** *tries to break the silence.*

ZOE: Dave-Ja-Vu. Funny.

CHLOE *gives her a look.* **HAYLEY** *realises she'd killed the mood and forcibly tries to cheer it back up.*

HAYLEY: If it's not sleeping bag then what is it?

CHLOE: Are you absolutely sure it wasn't sleepingbag?

LISA: It wasn't fucking sleepingbag!

ZOE: What were the letters again?

CHLOE: Samuel Beckett?

HAYLEY: Yeah, I'm sick of spying him out here at the peak of a Scottish mountain. That dead playwright gets everywhere, doesn't he?

CHLOE: Lisa's reading *Waiting for Godot*.

HAYLEY: I'll save you the effort. He doesn't turn up.

LISA: Spoilers!

HAYLEY: Ah, got it. Sarcastic Bitch!

LISA: Fuck sake it's just S!

CHLOE: Snow.

LISA: We have a winner! Your turn.

CHLOE: Shit. Didn't think of that.

> **RACHEL** *enters.*

RACHEL: Fuck me, it's cold out there.

ZOE: Over a week out here and it's still funny.

LISA: Good wee?

RACHEL: I've had better.

CHLOE: Not make it into the top ten?

RACHEL: Call me old fashioned, but my very best pisses usually don't involve me nearly freezing myself to a plastic fucking funnel.

HAYLEY: No one's forcing you to use it.

RACHEL: I should just drop my pants and piss, should I?

CHLOE: Squat first.

HAYLEY: We've all done it.

RACHEL: No chance. My arse gets cold.

CHLOE: Cold arse is the biggest killer round these parts.

LISA: Especially when it's the size of Rachel's.

HAYLEY: Squatting is better than just spraying and praying.

RACHEL: I'd be the expert.

LISA: Do you reckon guys know how lucky they are to have something they can actually point and aim?

CHLOE: You've never been in a guys' toilet have you?

LISA: Why would I?

RACHEL: I can think of a few reasons… *(She makes some vulgar gestures.)*

CHLOE: 'Aiming' isn't in their vocabulary.

LISA: You'd think they'd want the practice. If I had one, I'd be writing my name in the snow every chance I got.

RACHEL: And not for the first time Lisa's wishing she had a cock.

LISA: Pouring it out of a Shewee just isn't as satisfying.

CHLOE: I dunno what guys actually do, but it goes everywhere. Puddles on the floor, splashes up the wall. They must twirl it in their hands like a cane or something. It's disgusting.

HAYLEY: Ah, that's why Rachel has damp knees after nights out is it?

RACHEL: Something's gotta' soothe the carpet burns. You ever tried pissing in a urinal?

LISA: Oh god.

RACHEL: It's a fucking nightmare.

CHLOE: Why would you even try?

HAYLEY: You had to ask.

RACHEL: The ladies was closed for cleaning and I was ready to burst.

LISA: Use a cubicle?

RACHEL: Gents looked empty so I went in, undid, and kinda mounted it.

CHLOE: Face on?

RACHEL: I wasn't gonna sit in the fucking thing, was I? End up with one of those lemon things up my arse.

LISA: Cos that's exactly what would've happened.

RACHEL: So I'm on this thing and I've just started to let it flow.

CHLOE/HAYLEY: *(Singing vaguely to the tune of 'Let it Go') Let it flow, let it flow, can't hold this piss anymore…*

RACHEL: When in walks a guy and I can already hear him unzipping.

HAYLEY: And you're thinking 'fuck I'm missing the view'.

CHLOE/HAYLEY: *'Let it flow, let it flow, when a man walks through the door…'*

RACHEL: He walks right to the end urinal, gets his cock out, farts, then pisses like a gushing drain.

CHLOE: Funny coincidence; gushing drain was Rach's nickname at school.

CHLOE/HAYLEY: *'Here Rach stands mounting a bidet. Let the piss flow oooon….'*

ZOE: Is there a point to the story?

RACHEL: And you know what? Not once does he even glance at me.

CHLOE/HAYLEY: *'The man never bothered her anyway!'*

LISA: He's playing golf rules. Eyes on the ball.

RACHEL: He finishes, gobs and fucks off. Not a fucking word.

HAYLEY: Dirty bastard. Didn't wash his hands.

CHLOE: Rach, if I walked in on you mounting a urinal I'd not say anything either.

LISA: Maybe; 'On no, not again.'

RACHEL: Put me right off my wee.

CHLOE: Were you expecting him to offer you advice? 'No. What you're doing wrong sweetheart is you're getting all of this piss in the urinal. You need to splash more. Get it on your shoes.'

HAYLEY: Or maybe just lend a hand?

RACHEL: Fuck off. He was in his sixties.

CHLOE: You've had worse.

LISA: I'm sure you could've found some little blue pills somewhere.

CHLOE: There's vending machines on the walls.

HAYLEY: Poor bastard must've been terrified.

LISA: Why didn't you just piss in the sink?

RACHEL: And ruin my dignity?

LISA: We've all done it.

HAYLEY: Have we?

LISA: …Yes?

CHLOE/RACHEL/ZOE: …No.

HAYLEY: When have you pissed in a sink?

CHLOE: Where have you pissed in a sink?

LISA: Rachel mounted a urinal beside a pensioner – why am I the one being judged here?

RACHEL: How the tide turns. Time check anyone?

HAYLEY: What?

RACHEL: What time is it?

HAYLEY: You said time check. Who says time check?

RACHEL: Me. What's wrong with time check?

HAYLEY: What's wrong with 'what's the time?'

RACHEL: It's quicker.

CHLOE: By one word.

LISA: In a rush, are you?

CHLOE: Hot date.

LISA: Urinal man.

RACHEL: Fuck off. He had a face like a ball bag.

LISA: But ironically, his balls were totally wrinkle free.

CHLOE: You've never said 'Time Check' in your life.

RACHEL: I have.

CHLOE: When?

RACHEL: I say it all the time.

HAYLEY: Then start wearing a watch, it'll save you the effort.

RACHEL: Fuck sake, it's not that weird.

LISA: Nobody says time check.

ZOE: It's nearly six o'clock.

CHLOE: She's a mountaineer and explorer now. If Rachel wants to make herself sound cool by saying time check, we should let her.

RACHEL: You can all go fuck yourselves.

HAYLEY: Maybe later when I need warming up.

LISA: We're due a radio test at six.

CHLOE: Crap. Whose turn is it?

RACHEL: You can piss off if you think I'm going.

LISA: Decide quick.

HAYLEY: I know it's me, who's my buddy?

RACHEL: Not me.

CHLOE: I went last time.

ZOE: So did I.

RACHEL: There's no way it's my turn again. I've not warmed up yet from my pee.

CHLOE: Then you should go. Pointless us getting cold.

LISA: *(She makes a big show of reaching for her rucksack.)* Don't make me do it…

HAYLEY: Whoever it is, own up quick.

LISA: I'm reaching.

CHLOE: Rachel, if it's you just come clean.

RACHEL: If you've come clean then you've not come well.

ZOE: That's revolting.

LISA: Explains the state of your sleeping bag.

RACHEL: It's not me!

HAYLEY: It's fine, I'll go on my own.

CHLOE: You can't do that.

LISA: You know the rules. Pairs only. Last chance for someone to be a hero.

ZOE: I don't mind.

HAYLEY: Nobody should have to be a hero. Whoever it is should just fess up.

LISA: Just know whoever it is I'm not angry, I'm just disappointed. Very disappointed.

CHLOE: Rach, now look what you've done.

RACHEL: It's not my fucking turn!

> **LISA** *pulls a clipboard out of her rucksack. She's drawn up a schedule precisely to avoid these arguments. She consults the paper.*

LISA: Bollocks. It's me.

CHLOE: Oooh!

HAYLEY: Ouch.

RACHEL: Lisa, I'm not angry. I'm just really, really, really fucking disappointed in you.

HAYLEY: You haven't let us down. You've let yourself down.

LISA: There's no way I can spin this into being your fault, is there?

HAYLEY: Not a chance. But there is some rope in my bag if you want to, you know, go and do the decent thing. Or there's that knife somewhere, you can just slit your wrists.

This drops like a stone. For the first time, someone has gone too far. **ZOE** *in particular looks really upset. For the briefest of moments, nobody wants to say anything. Then, lightening the mood;*

RACHEL: Fucking. Dark. Shit.

LISA: The very definition of too soon.

RACHEL: Time?

HAYLEY: You mean time check?

RACHEL: Right. That's it. Find the knife.

LISA: It's after six. We're already late.

HAYLEY: Better get a move on or they'll be sounding the alarm.

RACHEL: Cos it'd be crap if a load of ripped mountain rescue guys turned up.

HAYLEY: We don't need rescued.

RACHEL: Who said anything about being rescued? I just need warmed up!

During this, **ZOE** *has crawled into her sleeping bag.* **CHLOE** *has moved over to sit with her.*

LISA: Then you can come with us. The walk will warm you up.

RACHEL: No chance, it's not my turn!

LISA indicates toward **CHLOE** *and* **ZOE**.

RACHEL: Shit. Everything okay?

CHLOE: *(Not looking up.)* Yeah. It'll be fine. Just went a bit far.

HAYLEY: Sorry. My fault.

CHLOE: Nobody's fault.

RACHEL: I should stay…

CHLOE: It's fine. Go. You'll not have washed your Shewee yet anyway.

RACHEL: And how the fuck do you know that you little pervert?

HAYLEY: You dirty bitch!

LISA: We'll just be five minutes. Unless you need…?

CHLOE: No worries. I've got things in here.

HAYLEY: Don't forget the radio.

RACHEL: Shout if you need anything.

> **LISA, HAYLEY** and **RACHEL** *leave the tent with the radio. The wind outside seems louder than ever.*

> **CHLOE** *sits with* **ZOE,** *who's almost fully retreated into the sleeping bag.*

CHLOE: We go too far sometimes. Don't let it get to you.

> **CHLOE** *gives* **ZOE** *a hug through the sleeping bag, and starts idly tidying the tent.*

ZOE: I'm sorry.

CHLOE: What for?

ZOE: I know I'm being stupid.

CHLOE: You're not being stupid.

ZOE: I shouldn't let it bother me.

CHLOE: Don't worry. You're with friends. We get it.

ZOE: You're with friends. I'm just the one tagging along.

CHLOE: Zoe, you're talking shit.

ZOE: Thanks. That's really encouraging.

CHLOE: We've been living together in a space the size of a shed for nearly two weeks. We're spooning each other for warmth at night. And we're sharing the same two Shewee's between five of us. We're eating, sleeping, walking and even shitting together. What more do you think needs to happen before you feel like you're part of the group?

ZOE: It's nothing you're doing. It's me. I know it's me.

CHLOE: If you're waiting for some initiation ceremony where we douse you in Rachel's piss and Lisa hands you control of the radio then you're going to be disappointed. That's not how friendships work. There's no off and on switch. You're here so you're one of us.

ZOE: You think that. The others don't.

CHLOE: They do.

ZOE: They hardly talk to me. And when they do they don't know what to say.

CHLOE: That's just in your head.

ZOE: Like just now. It was only awkward cos I'm here.

CHLOE: It was a stupid thing to say. It upset me too.

ZOE: Really?

CHLOE: They're my friends. They should know better.

ZOE: Exactly. They're <u>your</u> friends. They only let me come because of you.

CHLOE: That's bullshit and you know it. Everyone was welcome to tag along. It's a good cause, nobody was going to be left out.

ZOE: You're all so relaxed with each other. I stick out like a…

CHLOE: Spare dick in an orgy?

ZOE: I was going to say sore thumb.

CHLOE: You don't. You just need to try to get more on our wavelength. And I'll tell them they can tone it down.

ZOE: Don't.

CHLOE: They won't mind.

ZOE: Please.

CHLOE: You're doing fine. Friendships don't happen over night.

ZOE: They do for you. You've never had problems making friends.

CHLOE: I make an effort.

ZOE: It comes naturally to you.

CHLOE: You think?

ZOE: You thrive in company. You're a firework.

CHLOE: You can fuck off with the Katy Perry school of psychology. You gonna tell me everyone should hear me roar next?

ZOE: No…

CHLOE: Oh, so you meant after a bang I'm gone?

ZOE: See! You're quick and funny. You always know what to say. Whenever I try to speak up I'm too late. I don't think of the right thing to say until I'm at home replaying the day over in my head.

CHLOE: We're all like that. Nobody can say the right thing every time.

ZOE: I never do. Even my mum used to say I lived about half an hour behind everyone else.

CHLOE: I don't always know what to say. Nobody does. You just say something and hope for the best. If it doesn't land, who cares?

ZOE: Sometimes I'll replay the day again but with all the things I should've said. Take a second chance at getting it right.

CHLOE: Does it help?

ZOE: No. I just see new ways I've got it wrong. How I've managed to fuck up my life in a new and different way. You can polish a shit, but it's still a shit at the end of the day.

CHLOE: No one else sees it like that.

ZOE: And the ending is always the same. Me replaying things. Wishing I'd done it differently.

CHLOE: Nobody's judging you.

ZOE: They are. They won't admit it, but they are.

CHLOE: Then just judge them right back.

ZOE: What?

CHLOE: If that's how you feel then give as good as you get.

ZOE: I can't.

CHLOE: You can. Stop thinking you're an outsider, get stuck in and fuck the consequences.

ZOE: And how would you know?

CHLOE: Just jump in. You're the only one holding yourself back.

ZOE: I'll try.

CHLOE: And stop feeling so self-conscious. We're all in this together.

ZOE: Wait, how much of this advice has come straight from *High School Musical*?

CHLOE: It was either that or I was gonna start singing 'You've Got a Friend in Me'.

ZOE: Just general Disney based inspiration then?

> **CHLOE** *breaks into song with 'I'll Make A Man Out Of You' or something equally obtuse from the Disney songbook, as the action moves to outside the tent…*

OUTSIDE THE TENT

LISA *stands a distance away from the tent fiddling with the radio.* **RACHEL** *and* **HAYLEY** *watch on, looking cold.*

RACHEL: Did I mention it was fucking freezing?

HAYLEY: I think so. Do you want to say it again to be sure?

RACHEL: It's fucking freezing.

HAYLEY: Is she all right in there?

RACHEL: She'll be fine. Just needs some space.

HAYLEY: All the space in the world out here. We should swap. She can be freezing her tits off instead.

RACHEL: It's difficult. Having to watch what to say.

HAYLEY: I didn't think you'd noticed.

RACHEL: Cheeky bitch. I'm a sensitive person, me.

HAYLEY: Yeah, you're really toning it down.

RACHEL: Says Miss 'I'll just go slit my wrists.'

HAYLEY: I knew we should've had badges or something.

RACHEL: Saying what? 'BTW don't mention suicide'?

HAYLEY: 'Climbing Against Depression', 'Scaling For Suicide Prevention'. I don't know. Something to remind us why we're doing this. It could be something subtle.

RACHEL: Subtle is my middle name.

HAYLEY: Lucky you. Mine's Hilary.

RACHEL: Hayley Hilary? Bit of a mouthful.

HAYLEY: You'd know.

RACHEL: Don't nick my punchlines.

HAYLEY: Then don't be so obvious.

RACHEL: Not too obvious? Hmm. Okay. Topic at random… Paul.

HAYLEY: Don't go there.

RACHEL: Not too obvious was it?

HAYLEY: If I wanted to talk about it, I'd have done it by now.

RACHEL: And I've very generously given you all this time to dwell on it without asking, thank you very much.

HAYLEY: You don't think I'd have chucked it out as a topic during one of the long silences if I actually wanted to talk about it?

RACHEL: Not with those nosy bitches chipping in. But it's just you and me and I'm not waiting any longer. So come on. Spill.

HAYLEY: I'm not having this conversation. I don't want it.

RACHEL: You won't. It's shit. Which is exactly why you need to let it out. Holding in a big shit only makes it worse, trust me. I'm an expert.

HAYLEY: *(To* **LISA***.)* Are you finished pissing about with that radio yet?

RACHEL: I can wait here all day.

HAYLEY: For what? For me to tell you he was a shitbag, a creep and a two-timing fuck? What's the point? That's not news to you. You were there. You know exactly what he was.

RACHEL: Do I?

HAYLEY: I knew it. I fucking knew it. You're just like the rest of them. You're on his side.

RACHEL: Whoah now, don't be starting with that shit. You know that's not true.

HAYLEY: So what's all this for then, waiting till we're at the top of a mountain to bring it up? What stupid hot take have you been waiting all this time to share?

RACHEL: Show me your arm.

HAYLEY: What?

RACHEL: Show me your arm.

HAYLEY: It's cold. I'll freeze, you nutcase.

RACHEL: Hayley, I'll pin you down in the snow and rip that fucking jacket off you if you don't roll up your sleeve right now.

HAYLEY *stops fighting and shows her upper arm. There's a fairly fresh cut surrounded by an array of much older scars.*

RACHEL: Fuck.

HAYLEY: Sorry.

RACHEL: No don't you start apologising, you'll make me feel shit.

HAYLEY: Sorry.

RACHEL: See!

HAYLEY: I could tell you I cut myself shaving if it helps.

RACHEL: I thought you'd stopped. That the sessions helped.

HAYLEY: I had. And they did. But it's been a while, and I started again. Just the one. Snapped the zip tag off my sleeping bag and scratched.

RACHEL: Am I allowed to ask why?

HAYLEY: Well it's nothing you did if that's what you're worried about. The shite you say makes me want to hurt you, not myself.

RACHEL: Thanks.

HAYLEY: Anytime. It was a few nights ago. When Lisa said about googling Mark 'for research' before going on their date.

RACHEL: We all do a little cyberstalking first. Only natural. If they wanna fill their 'gram up with pictures it's only fair we're allowed a quick perv.

HAYLEY: Yeah we do. Only natural. Except that's when I realised I'd gone nine days without looking at Paul's. So what? Who cares! But that's the longest I've ever gone since I've known him.

RACHEL: You're still checking him out?

HAYLEY: Because he could be doing anything. Literally anything. And I'd not know. I mean he's probably with Katie, that's all he's been doing since they got together. But I hated not knowing for sure. And worse I hated myself for caring.

RACHEL: So you cut?

HAYLEY: Because why am I not over him? He's a complete dick! Why can't I let him go?

RACHEL: Sounds like you're still waiting for closure.

HAYLEY: No, I can't claim that excuse. I got closure, trust me. We meet up, he dumps me and I tell him that I love him.

RACHEL: Why didn't you just tell me? We could've talked about it. Or gone and fucked him up. You didn't need to do that…

HAYLEY: No, I didn't. I wasn't thinking rationally so I did an irrational thing. Can't fault my logic.

RACHEL: There's not a guy on earth worth that.

She gives her a hug.

HAYLEY: Don't tell the others.

RACHEL: I won't. Do I need to hide all of our sharp objects?

HAYLEY: Only for your own safety.

RACHEL: I'm serious.

HAYLEY: Me too.

*   **LISA** *rushes past them brandishing the radio. It's emitting bursts of static followed by a series of three bleeps.*

LISA: The radio's fucked.

HAYLEY: Fantastic. Today just keeps getting better.

They all head back inside the tent.

INSIDE THE TENT

ZOE *is out of the sleeping bag.* **CHLOE** *is still tidying up.* **LISA**, **RACHEL** *and* **HAYLEY** *enter. The radio is still crackling with static and sporadically spitting out electronic beeps.*

LISA: Everything okay?

ZOE: Yeah. Sorry about that.

CHLOE: Just a little wobble. We're good.

LISA: Awesome. Cos we've a new problem.

ZOE: What was the old problem?

CHLOE: What's Rachel done this time?

RACHEL: Why do you assume it's me?

ZOE: It's always you!

CHLOE: You're the one who broke the tent pole…

ZOE: Lost the matches…

CHLOE: Tore the rucksack strap…

ZOE: Ripped the map…

CHLOE: Spilt water on Hayley's sleeping bag.

HAYLEY: That was you?

RACHEL: Well I *said* it was water…

The radio gives a sudden and very loud burst of static.

HAYLEY: What the hell was that?

RACHEL: Fuck, we nearly had another accident!

LISA: The radio's fucked. I've been trying to signal our position but I'm just getting static.

ZOE: That's not good.

HAYLEY: Well you're obviously doing it wrong.

LISA: I've managed fine for the last ten days, thank you.

HAYLEY: You've just pressed something. Give it here.

LISA: You're a radio expert now, are you?

HAYLEY: No. But technology is all the same. If it's broken you switch it off and switch it back on again.

*She grabs the radio from **LISA**.*

HAYLEY: How do you turn it off?

LISA: Give it here.

She turns it off. They all stare expectantly.

CHLOE: Now what?

LISA: We need to leave it off for ten seconds before restarting it.

All eyes are on the radio. They're all counting ten seconds in their heads.

ZOE: Ten! Sorry.

RACHEL: Switch it back on then.

HAYLEY: Don't we need a time check first?

RACHEL: How did I fucking know that was coming?

> **LISA** *switches the radio on. It bleeps a few brief notes as it powers up.*

CHLOE: What does that mean?

LISA: That it's turning on.

RACHEL: Can't it do it any quicker?

LISA: You're welcome to ask it.

RACHEL: Hurry up, you slow fuck!

> *It finishes bleeping. Silence for a moment, then the static once again.*

LISA: Shit.

CHLOE: Now what do we do?

HAYLEY: Off and on again?

CHLOE: Did you press something and lose the frequency?

LISA: I've been cycling through all the bands mountain rescue gave us but I'm not getting anything. It's just static.

RACHEL: Anyone else find all this tech talk kinda hot?

ZOE: Maybe it's the snow?

HAYLEY: Can we cope without it?

LISA: They said in case of radio failure we should stay put and they could pick us up from our last known location.

CHLOE: Does that mean we're done? It's over?

ZOE: No!

CHLOE: All that money we raised. If we don't reach the peak what are we supposed to do, give it back?

RACHEL: No, no. no. We're not giving up just because some fucking radio decides to go to shit.

LISA: Nobody said anything about giving up. We're not quitting and we're not getting rescued. We stay here for now and we keep checking in. Whatever's wrong will right itself. It's probably the weather or something.

HAYLEY: That actually sounded convincing.

LISA: I'm not just a pretty face.

HAYLEY: Good job really.

CHLOE: So. What do we do while we wait?

LISA: Well… There's always eye spy.

RACHEL: Fuck that for a barrel of monkeys. It's time for Plan B.

HAYLEY: What happened to Plan A?

LISA: She suggested Plan A back on night two. We turned her down.

CHLOE: The orgy?

RACHEL: You were all complaining you were cold. Quickest way to warm up!

HAYLEY: That coming from experience, is it?

RACHEL: Experience helps with the 'coming', but it's not essential. You'll all pick it up quickly enough.

LISA: I've always wondered what the etiquette is at an orgy. Do you introduce yourself first or just get stuck in?

RACHEL: Always wondered? Bit of a secret kink? Well if you're lucky, tonight you might find out!

HAYLEY: How do you choose where to start? Is there a set orgy menu or is it more of a nibble what you fancy buffet?

RACHEL: Different sort of finger food.

ZOE: Finger licking good!

CHLOE: That's gross.

RACHEL: We'll shelve Plan A for now then. I want to keep my energy up for mountain rescue.

HAYLEY: They'll take no time scaling her peaks. So orgy's off the table for now.

RACHEL: Keeping it in the drawer for another day. No better way to celebrate our success.

LISA: Except for the feeling of personal triumph and all that money raised for charity.

RACHEL: Fuck that. I want to be the first person to climax at the top of the Yapstovals.

CHLOE: That'll be the title of her autobiography.

HAYLEY: If Rachel is already planning our victory celebration, I won't need to save this…

She pulls a bottle of vodka out of her sleeping bag.

CHLOE: Nice!

RACHEL: You've been hiding that in there all this time? Cheeky minx! No wonder you weren't keen on letting me crawl in with you.

HAYLEY: Who's up for a drinking game to pass the time?

CHLOE: Yay!

RACHEL: Would it not be easier just to down it and get shit faced?

ZOE: It's not really my thing.

LISA: I don't see what any of us has to gain playing spin the bottle.

RACHEL: Not really a drinking game but if you're that desperate for a cheeky snog don't be shy. Don't hide behind the bottle.

LISA: One day someone's going to call you out on your bullshit.

RACHEL: Bullshit? You think? Come here!

She makes a big show of getting really close to **LISA***, expecting her to pull away.* **LISA** *doesn't move.* **RACHEL** *hesitates.*

LISA: Told you!

She gives her a quick peck. **RACHEL** *retreats.* **CHLOE** *starts handing out cups.* **ZOE***, pointedly, shakes her head, not wanting one.*

ZOE: So what are we playing then?

CHLOE: Never have I ever!

HAYLEY: Good call.

LISA: I've managed to avoid that one so far.

CHLOE: Fun, funny and really easy to get Rachel pissed. We say something we've never done and if anyone's done it, they drink.

HAYLEY: Jesus, Rachel's gonna drown.

RACHEL: Oi!

CHLOE: Since you've not played before, you can start us off.

LISA: Okay, easy. I've never played…

HAYLEY: You're supposed to say 'never have I ever' first.

LISA: Why?

CHLOE: Cos it's fun.

LISA: Is it?

RACHEL: Fucks sake, hurry up some of us are thirsty.

LISA: Never have I ever played this game before.

Everyone drinks.

CHLOE: Never have I ever… peed in the shower.

Everyone but **HAYLEY** *drinks.*

LISA: Seriously? It's bliss!

RACHEL: Pissing standing up with none of the consequences.

CHLOE: You're peeing down yourself, it's disgusting.

RACHEL: It's only disgusting if there's someone else in with you. Unless they asked for it.

HAYLEY: Never have I ever… Invited a guy back for Netflix and Chill.

LISA and RACHEL drink.

CHLOE: I don't have Netflix.

HAYLEY: I'm more an Amazon Prime and Dine girl.

CHLOE: Better than 'Now TV, it's just me'.

LISA: I don't get the 'Netflix and Chill' thing. Sounds like he wants to watch the telly and drink a hot chocolate.

CHLOE: I thought it was a warning – the guy is really telling you 'come home with me and you'll be lying on your back binging a box set over my shoulder'.

RACHEL: Never have I ever… Saved a nude on my phone.

Everyone drinks.

RACHEL: Right. Let's see them!

HAYLEY: You seriously saying you haven't?

RACHEL: You want to see me pose sexy you just need to ask.

ZOE: Never have I ever…

A sudden loud burst of static comes from the radio. Underneath the heavy static is what could be a voice, but it's impossible to make out.

LISA: Jesus! I forgot that was on.

RACHEL: If it does that one more fucking time I'm chucking it off a ledge!

ZOE: At least we know it's working.

LISA: There's definitely something coming through. We need to take it outside to reduce the interference.

CHLOE: I'll come with you. I haven't stretched my legs yet. And if I stay in here any longer I run the risk of feeling warm.

LISA and **CHLOE** *exit with the radio.* **RACHEL** *and* **HAYLEY** *finish their drinks and pour another.* **ZOE** *busies herself to avoid being asked.*

ZOE: I'll go make sure everything's okay.

She exits.

HAYLEY: My turn to ask a question.

RACHEL: Is it where do babies come from?

HAYLEY: You raised over twice as much money as the rest of us combined.

RACHEL: You see, when a mummy and a daddy love each other very much they call for the stork to come round and give mummy a good pounding, then nine months later…

HAYLEY: Were you shagging around for the charity money?

RACHEL: Fuck off. I'm not a goodwill prostitute.

HAYLEY: Over three grand? People are generous when it's for a good cause, but nobody can raise three grand for a charity hike up a big hill.

RACHEL: I know generous people.

HAYLEY: To the tune of three thousand pounds?

RACHEL: Yeah.

HAYLEY: Who?

RACHEL: None of your business.

HAYLEY: Don't make me play my 'told you about my ex issues' card already. I was hoping I'd have that in my back pocket for a while.

RACHEL: My parents' church friends, okay? Everyone donated. Every single one of them. They're generous.

HAYLEY: I didn't know you were religious.

RACHEL: I'm not. They are.

HAYLEY: Right. And that's not touching a nerve at all.

RACHEL: Are your parents religious?

HAYLEY: No. We say happy birthday Jesus every Christmas and stand up for the Queen, but that's about it.

RACHEL: Then you don't know. So shut the fuck up.

HAYLEY: Apple fell far from the tree, I see. Explains a lot.

RACHEL: Don't fucking start your bullshitty psychoanalysis. You have no idea.

HAYLEY: I'm not judging. Believe whatever you want to believe.

RACHEL: Believe what I want? I fucking wish! Until I came to Uni I wasn't given a choice. I was given the Bible. The actual words of God. The truth. That's what I was told I had to believe.

HAYLEY: Heavy stuff.

RACHEL: Ever read it?

HAYLEY: No. Think I understand the basics though. God. Jesus. Love. Loaves and fishes. Died for our sins. I've heard there's a bit about a talking donkey and some haemorrhoid curses, but that might've been someone taking the piss.

RACHEL reaches into her rucksack and pulls out a pocket edition of the Bible. It's well thumbed. She throws it to HAYLEY.

RACHEL: Take a look for yourself.

HAYLEY: You carry it with you? Rachel, you never fail to surprise me.

RACHEL: Want to be really impressed? Genesis Chapter One, Verse One: In the beginning God created the heaven and the earth. And the earth was without form, and void; and darkness was upon the face of the deep. And the Spirit of God moved upon the face of the waters. And God said, Let there be light: and there was light. And God saw the light, that it was good: and God divided the light from the darkness. And God called the light Day, and the darkness he called Night. And the evening and the morning were the first day.

HAYLEY: Word perfect. I can do the same with Lewis Carol's *Jabberwocky*. "Twas brillig and the slithy toves did gyre and gimble in the wabe…" Makes about as much sense as Genesis.

RACHEL: It's not just the first page. Flip to anything early in the Old Testament. I get ropey beyond Joshua. Just give me gospel and chapter.

HAYLEY: Leviticus 12.

RACHEL: Jehovah went on to say to Moses: "Tell the Israelites, 'If a woman becomes pregnant and gives birth to a male, she will be unclean for seven days, just as she is in the days of the impurity when she is menstruating. On the eighth day, the flesh of his foreskin will be circumcised. She will continue cleansing herself from the blood for the next 33 days. She should not touch any holy thing, and she should not come into the holy place until she fulfils the days of her purification."

HAYLEY: I don't even know where to start pulling that apart.

RACHEL: Don't. It's bullshit. But if you want the 'How To Guide', you'll need this too.

She hunts out a copy of 'The Watchtower' magazine from her bag.

HAYLEY: Is this what I think it is?

RACHEL: Yeah. More bullshit.

HAYLEY: You're the last person on Earth I'd have thought would be a Jehovah's Witness.

RACHEL: I think it's pretty fucking clear I'm not.

HAYLEY: Ex-Witness then. Silent Witness. Witness protection.

RACHEL: You have no fucking idea.

OUTSIDE THE TENT

LISA *and* **CHLOE** *are fiddling with the radio. There's lots of static, but something lurking underneath it all.*

LISA: I'm not going mad, there's definitely something there?

CHLOE: I think so.

LISA: I'll keep trying. One more scan through all the frequencies just in case.

CHLOE: You're such a geek.

Pause.

CHLOE: You weren't drinking.

LISA: What?

CHLOE: You weren't drinking during the game. You put the mug to your lips but didn't drink.

LISA: Well spotted.

CHLOE: Not a vodka fan?

LISA: You could say that.

CHLOE: It's not my favourite. Comes back a bit too quickly. But I think popping prosecco corks might've been a bit impractical.

LISA: True.

CHLOE: Not as much fun to chug either. The bubbles go up your nose.

LISA: Mmm.

Pause. **ZOE** *joins them.*

ZOE: Any progress out here?

CHLOE: Still nothing.

LISA: Doesn't sound like it.

CHLOE: You didn't need to, you know.

LISA: Didn't need to?

CHLOE: Pretend to drink. You could've just said no.

LISA: Yes. I could.

CHLOE: But you didn't.

LISA: No.

CHLOE: Okay.

Pause.

CHLOE: Why not?

LISA: Do you really want to know, or are you just asking to fill the awkward silence.

CHLOE: A little from column A, a little from column B.

LISA: I thought so.

Pause.

CHLOE: I am curious though.

Pause.

ZOE: Me too. First time I've ever felt braver than any of you.

Pause.

CHLOE: Eye spy with my little eye...

LISA: You get labelled if you don't drink. You're a 'non drinker.'

CHLOE: What's wrong with that?

LISA: It's the only thing you're labelled for not doing. People aren't called non drug addicts. Non cyclists. Non bungee jumpers. You have a choice whether you want to do something or not. So why do people get to judge you for something you're not doing.

ZOE: Nobody's judging you.

CHLOE: They're just jealous of your willpower.

LISA: They're all thinking the same thing... Why? Why doesn't she drink. As though there must be something wrong with her. Everybody drinks, so why doesn't Lisa? She's flawed or she's broken. Something must be missing.

CHLOE: Who cares what people think? People judge people all the time. We judge them right back for judging us.

LISA: Because of course there's a reason. I know why I don't drink. But who can be arsed to have that conversation over and over again. Met with the same apologetic looks. The same patronising smiles. It's easier to pretend.

CHLOE: I'm sorry.

LISA: And now I've upset you talking about why I don't talk about it. *(Pause.)* It's the snow. Can't help but be a little self-reflective.

CHLOE: Geek.

Through the static they briefly hear the numbers 5. 14. before losing the signal again.

ZOE: There! You had something.

LISA: That was definitely something…

Long pause as she works through the radio frequencies. Fleetingly the numbers are heard, but too garbled to understand. Eventually she finds a reasonably clear signal.

The numbers should now be audible, but still shrouded in static. It's a disturbingly monotone voice – an actual person, not a computer synth – but clearly a recording. It plays on repeat.

24. 9. 19. 20.

Beep. Beep. Beep.

19. 14. 15. 23. 13. 5. 14. Beep. 5. 24. 9. 19. 20.

Beep. Beep. Beep.

19. 14. 15. 23

LISA: What the hell is going on?

ZOE: No. No this isn't right!

ZOE runs back toward the tent. CHLOE shouts after her.

CHLOE: Zoe!

LISA: Zoe?

CHLOE: This is seriously creepy.

LISA: Let's get back inside. We need to show the others.

They enter the tent. The numbers continue to play in the loop. The sound of the wind has now been completely replaced by static.

INSIDE THE TENT

HAYLEY *and* **RACHEL** *are sat as before.* **ZOE** *rushes in, swiftly followed by* **CHLOE** *and* **LISA**. **HAYLEY** *passes* **RACHEL** *her Bible back, who slips it into her sleeping bag without anyone spotting it. The radio continues to play the number loop.*

LISA: We've got a serious problem.

RACHEL: Fan-fucking-tastic. I was just starting to think today was going too well.

ZOE *is back in her corner, clearly freaked out by all of this. As ever,* **CHLOE** *has gone over to check she's okay.*

ZOE: We shouldn't be here!

HAYLEY: What's wrong now?

CHLOE: It's fine, don't worry.

RACHEL: At least you've got the radio working.

LISA: We haven't. That's the problem.

RACHEL: So what's that then?

LISA: We have no idea. Listen.

They let the current cycle play to the end then listen to the whole thing through. As the scene progresses everyone is going to become influenced by these numbers, each developing their own little tick or twitch. These start very subtly but steadily build as the scene continues.

ZOE *is the only one not affected, though initially she's in her own world and doesn't notice.*

RACHEL: Numbers repeating over and over? Fuck. We've ended up in an episode of *Lost!*

HAYLEY: Well I was having a lovely time and now haven't a clue what's going on, so yeah, maybe we have!

CHLOE: Why did it end with them all in a church?

ZOE: They were all dead!

CHLOE: Spoilers!

RACHEL: The first few seasons were great, then it just started going batshit crazy for no reason.

HAYLEY: What did the numbers mean in the end?

RACHEL: Pretty sure they were lottery winning numbers.

HAYLEY: Shit, someone write them down then!

CHLOE: They were just mysterious magic numbers. They didn't bother explaining them.

ZOE: They were cursed.

LISA: I think we've more important priorities right now than a shitty old TV show.

RACHEL: Sawyer though.

LISA: I'm serious. We need to sort this.

HAYLEY: Does the voice sound familiar?

LISA: Should it?

HAYLEY: I dunno. I'm not sure.

RACHEL: It's distorted, it could be anyone.

CHLOE: One of the mountain rescue guys playing a joke?

LISA: I'll kill them if it is.

She speaks into the radio.

LISA: Ha-ha guys very funny. You got us.

Still the same pattern repeats.

LISA: Seriously this stopped being funny really quickly.

RACHEL: It wasn't fucking funny to start with.

LISA: Whatever it is, it's completely blocking out the signal.

HAYLEY: Really, does no one else think they recognise the voice?

CHLOE: It's just playing the same thing over and over… *(She joins in reciting the numbers from their current position.)*

ZOE: Please. Please don't do that.

LISA: That's really fucked up Chloe. Stop.

CHLOE: Sorry.

No one knows quite what to do. The cycle repeats several times with everyone's twitches becoming slightly more pronounced.

HAYLEY: I swear I know that voice.

RACHEL: *Lost* might actually have the answer…

LISA: Really? You going to turn into a smoke monster or a polar bear?

RACHEL: They didn't explain the numbers but they did explain where they came from. That hatch thing.

LISA: Ah. So it's not magic numbers, just a secret, evil cult base hidden beneath us. Anyone spotted a secret hatch in the last few days? Did we pitch our tent on top of the thing?

RACHEL: Shut up and fucking listen to me. It was based on a real thing. I'm sure it was.

CHLOE: A numbers station.

RACHEL: That's it!

HAYLEY: What the fuck is a numbers station?

CHLOE: A transmitter that just repeats the same thing over and over again. They were used for spying and codes and things years ago.

RACHEL: And when exactly did you end up a Lisa level nerd on this bullshit?

CHLOE: There's only so many YouTube cat videos you can watch before it starts auto-playing the creepy shit.

LISA: And you think there's one of these things at the top of a random fucking Scottish mountain? Do you think they need to do much spying up here?

RACHEL: Listen to the message, what the fuck else do you think it could be?

HAYLEY: Is it seriously just me? Does really no one else recognise that fucking voice?

CHLOE: I'm just saying Rachel could be right. It could be a numbers station.

LISA: But there was nothing on this frequency yesterday? Why would it suddenly change, it doesn't make any sense.

RACHEL: This is all so fucked up.

ZOE: What else could it be?

LISA: Okay. Let's say for a second this is a 'numbers station' then the message must be a code, yeah?

CHLOE: Probably, yeah.

LISA: So let's crack it.

RACHEL: What do you know about cracking codes? Or do you watch as much internet bullshit as Chloe?

CHLOE: It might have been broadcasting since the 1950s and it was designed to be unbreakable, we'll never decode it.

ZOE: I don't want to know.

LISA: If it's a message, I want to know what it's saying.

ZOE: We should just turn it off.

CHLOE: I think that's probably a good idea.

HAYLEY: Seriously, forget the numbers for a second and just listen to the voice!

RACHEL: Hayley shut the fuck up, nobody recognises the voice!

LISA: The most basic code is substitution. Replacing one thing with another.

She grabs paper out of her rucksack and starts writing down the code.

RACHEL: I've had enough of this.

She reaches for the radio.

LISA: Don't you fucking dare.

CHLOE: Can we just turn it off? Something's definitely not right.

HAYLEY: Not until we've figured out who the fuck it is.

LISA: And what they're saying. The most obvious substitution would be replacing each number with its corresponding letter of the alphabet…

She draws up a grid. While she's distracted **RACHEL** *grabs the radio.*

RACHEL: I don't know what the fuck's up with everyone, but I'm stopping this now.

She changes the frequency. It squeaks and crackles but then continues to play the repeating cycle of numbers.

HAYLEY: Leave it the fuck alone!

HAYLEY *reaches for the radio, but* **RACHEL** *pulls away. She begins flipping through the various frequencies at speed. Each time it's still playing the same cycle.*

RACHEL: What the fuck?

CHLOE *takes the radio from her. She has a little more expertise and flips through the frequencies slower and more deliberately. And is it their imagination or are the numbers getting louder?*

CHLOE: It's on every frequency.

HAYLEY: I know that voice!

LISA: Got it! A simple number/letter substitute. A is one, B is two, C is three.

RACHEL: So what does it say?

LISA: Snowmen Exist…

The numbers are now definitely louder. It's almost uncomfortable.

ZOE: Turn it off.

LISA: We've solved it. We can turn it off.

HAYLEY: Turn it off.

RACHEL: Chloe for fuck's sake turn it off!

    CHLOE *flicks the on/off button but it makes no difference.*

CHLOE: I'm trying! It won't!

ZOE: Turn it off!

LISA: Just turn it off!

HAYLEY: You need to turn it off.

RACHEL: Turn the fucking thing off!

CHLOE: *(Shouting above the cacophony.)* IT WON'T TURN OFF!

HAYLEY: Then break it.

RACHEL: Smash it.

LISA: Throw it outside.

ZOE: Kill it!

    CHLOE *smashes the radio against the ground and it breaks apart. The silence is immediate and monstrous. The girls are now all silent and motionless, except for their twitches.* **ZOE** *stands among them, the only one seemingly conscious of what's going on.*

ZOE: Guys? Come on snap out of it. Guys can you hear me? We need to go. Right now. Guys come on, please. Don't do this to me. Don't leave me alone again.

Please…

Slow fade to blackout with **ZOE** *surrounded by madness.*

INSIDE THE TENT

The bleeping of the numbers returns, instantly transforming into the bleeping of **LISA***'s alarm clock. Everyone is tucked up in their sleeping bags except* **ZOE** *who's already up. The remains of the radio are still lying where it was smashed.*

ZOE: Wakey-wakey, rise and shine.

HAYLEY: Morning already?

CHLOE: No. Can't be.

RACHEL: What time is it?

LISA: Excuse me?

RACHEL: What time is it?

LISA: No, I don't think so.

HAYLEY: Lisa, can I have a 'time check' please.

LISA: Of course you can, Hayley. It's 7.45am.

RACHEL: You're all bitches and I should've killed you while you slept.

CHLOE: Is the kettle on?

ZOE: No, sorry, I didn't want to risk waking anyone.

HAYLEY: Alright, I can take the hint. Give me a minute.

They each start to get up and ready themselves for the day – brushing teeth, changing inside the sleeping bag, etc. It's abundantly clear that a lot is going unsaid. Nobody quite knows how to bring it up. At great length, **ZOE** *decides to shoulder the burden.*

ZOE: So. Are we going to talk about last night then or are we just going to ignore it?

CHLOE: The silence had to break eventually.

Everyone looks at her.

HAYLEY: Yeah.

CHLOE: So. What the hell was last night about?

LISA: Bad vodka.

ZOE: What?

LISA: Has to be. It's the only thing that makes sense. What percent was it?

HAYLEY: Oi, I only buy the best…

She rummages in her sleeping bag and pulls out the bottle.

HAYLEY: …miscellaneous foreign vodka that doesn't even have numbers in English.

RACHEL: It's probably fucking paint stripper, no wonder we were all off our heads.

ZOE: Explains why it didn't affect me. Sober for the win!

HAYLEY: It does smell pretty rancid in the cold light of day.

LISA: There we go. We were fucked off our faces on Hayley's finest Albanian import.

CHLOE: *(Pointedly, to **LISA**.)* You're sure about that, are you?

LISA: Very. It explains everything.

RACHEL: Good. Cos I was getting seriously worried we'd all finally fucking lost it.

*The tension is broken. Now they can laugh about it. Except **CHLOE**.*

LISA: Creepy as hell!

RACHEL: Fucking terrifying!

HAYLEY: A little bit of wee actually came out, not gonna lie.

LISA: Only a little bit? I'm going to have to burn my pants.

HAYLEY: Why is the human body's response to fear to want to piss or shit yourself? That's just bad design.

LISA: Doesn't really help with fight or flight, does it?

HAYLEY: Fight, flight or faeces.

LISA: Is it even possible to run and pee at the same time?

RACHEL: A big shit could make a pretty decent weapon.

ZOE: Rachel!

RACHEL: It could! Who's gonna come at you when you're holding a big steaming shit in your hand?

LISA: Steaming?!

RACHEL: It's called shit hot for a reason.

HAYLEY: I'd take creepy numbers over a shit-smeared Rachel any day.

RACHEL: I didn't say smeared.

LISA: So maybe the body does know what it's doing. Get scared. Shit yourself. Make a mess. Whatever's scared you goes 'I'm not fucking touching that!' And leaves you alone.

RACHEL: Can't wait to read the Lisa Cochran survival guide.

LISA: Reviewers say it's both shit hot and hot shit. Reserve your copy today!

HAYLEY: Those numbers though.

RACHEL: Fucking mental.

HAYLEY: I love how we overhear some weird creepy numbers and we're all scared shitless…

LISA: Shitless now? We were full of shit before – get it right.

CHLOE: This isn't funny.

RACHEL: It kinda is.

HAYLEY: All these random numbers and Leese jumps straight to 'Well it must be a code!'

ZOE: Sherlock-ran over there.

RACHEL: Twelve – months of the year. Two – Kit-Kats come in twos so that's something to do with cat years…

HAYLEY: My first is in whistle but not in canoe.

LISA: It was worth a guess.

CHLOE: She was right. There was a message.

HAYLEY: Bet you used to add up boyfriends' phone numbers and compare totals to see if it was real love.

LISA: Shame you didn't do that with Paul's.

ZOE: BURN!

CHLOE: But there was a message.

RACHEL: Yeah, from the spooky fucking 'numbers station'.

LISA: A numbers station! Where did we even get that from?

HAYLEY: I bet one of us was humming the *Lost* theme tune during the last climb.

RACHEL: Did *Lost* even have a theme?

LISA: No it was more a kinda *(She delivers her best version of the Lost opening.)*

HAYLEY: You know what I mean. Something stupid will have put the idea in our heads.

RACHEL: Fucking *Lost*. Of all the weird shit to spring to mind.

LISA: I stopped watching after they killed the hobbit.

HAYLEY: There were hobbits in it?

LISA: Just one.

HAYLEY: With hairy feet?

LISA: He wasn't playing a hobbit, num-nutts.

HAYLEY: Num-nutts is a pretty good hobbit name.

ZOE: Frodo was the worst.

LISA: I bet you a fiver those numbers turn out to be for a takeaway restaurant or something.

HAYLEY: Shit. Do you think we hacked Just Eat?

RACHEL: I wish. I'm fucking starving.

LISA: And instead of placing an order for some won-tons and crackers…

HAYLEY: And some satay chicken sticks.

LISA: We all flip out and let Chloe break the radio.

RACHEL: Yeah, nice one Chloe.

CHLOE: You all told me to!

LISA: All because we were all too pissed to remember how to switch the thing off.

ZOE: Makes sense.

CHLOE: I'm going out for some air.

    CHLOE *exits the tent.*

RACHEL: Who pissed in her cheerios?

HAYLEY: She probably feels guilty for smashing it. Wasn't her fault.

LISA: She's struggling. It's all getting to her more than she lets on. You've seen what she's like.

HAYLEY: I'll go.

LISA: No. Give her some time to herself. It'll do her good.

ZOE: I don't think you're being very fair.

HAYLEY: I forget she knew her better than the rest of us.

RACHEL: Not really. Everyone just feels closer to Chloe cos she's just so damn adorable.

LISA: Jealous much?

RACHEL: Too fucking right!

ZOE: It's nice though, to be friendly with everyone. If it wasn't for her I'd not be here.

LISA: Did you ever put that kettle on?

ZOE: Shit, no. Sorry. I thought Hayley…

HAYLEY: I'm going. I'm going…

HAYLEY *exits.*

LISA: Do you regret signing up for this?

ZOE: No. Not at all.

RACHEL: Nah. There's been some shit bits. Lots of actual, literal shit bits.

LISA: Weird when a toilet seat becomes the thing you miss most.

RACHEL: I'm sick of being cold, I'm gagging for a proper shag. Or at least a wank where I can give myself the attention I deserve and not have to keep it down for you lot.

LISA: That's you keeping it down? I'd be worried about friction burns.

RACHEL: I can show you my technique if you like?

LISA: Okay. I'm game. Show me.

ZOE doesn't know where to look. She grabs the Shewee.

ZOE: Pee time, I think!

She exits hurriedly. **LISA** *has locked eyes with* **RACHEL** *and moves towards her.*

LISA: Come on, Rachel. Show me. I'm eager to learn.

RACHEL: You on the turn?

LISA: Won't know 'til I've tried.

RACHEL: Good. First you warm your hands up. Anything cold contracts the blood vessels. Less blood, less feeling. Less feeling, less fun.

LISA: I'm hearing a lot of talk. You said you were going to show me.

RACHEL: Setting the tone is half the battle. I'm not offering any old quick angry wank here. This is satisfaction guaranteed.

LISA is now very close to RACHEL. It's the same game as last time, but RACHEL's determined not to be the one to break. LISA breathes on her hands and takes RACHEL's hands in hers.

LISA: Warm enough?

RACHEL: They'll do. But don't go straight for the kill.

LISA: No?

RACHEL: No. Savour your hand on its long journey to destination O.

LISA: You're stalling.

RACHEL: I'm making you work for it.

LISA: You're not as easy as I thought.

RACHEL: Bitch. My body is a temple. I don't allow just anyone inside my pearly gates.

> **LISA** *slides her hand down inside* **RACHEL**'s *sleeping bag.* **RACHEL** *almost dare not move. She could break at any second.*

LISA: There's something special inside here. Something I've been waiting to get my hands on for a very long time…

> *She's now reaching so far inside she's practically lying on top of* **RACHEL**. **LISA** *moves as though she's about to kiss her.*

RACHEL: *(All pretence gone.)* Lisa, I don't…

LISA: This!

> *She pulls* **RACHEL**'s *Bible out from the sleeping bag.*

RACHEL: You fucking bitch.

LISA: Sorry. You're just not my type.

RACHEL: Hayley wasn't supposed to say anything.

LISA: She didn't. I've heard you whispering to yourself after you thought we'd all fallen sleep.

RACHEL: So you've been spying on me.

LISA: I thought at first you were going to your happy place. I could hear you saying 'Oh God' a lot.

RACHEL: Fuck you.

LISA: No reason to be embarrassed. I just wasn't expecting to hear you praying, that's all.

OUTSIDE THE TENT

CHLOE *is pacing, angry.* **HAYLEY** *is quietly sorting the fire to get the water boiling.*

HAYLEY: Let it out. You'll feel better.

CHLOE: I don't think so.

HAYLEY: It helps. I learned the hard way; keep things bottled up for too long and the lid gets stuck.

CHLOE: Is this life advice or just good tupperware management?

HAYLEY: Both. I'm amazingly multipurpose.

CHLOE: You don't really believe it was bad vodka?

HAYLEY: It makes sense. And it was really, really cheap vodka. My Albanian isn't great but I think I've now taught myself the word for 'Turps'.

CHLOE: I didn't feel drunk.

HAYLEY: We hadn't had anything proper to drink since, what, night five when we finished your rum?

CHLOE: How did we manage to walk the next day?

HAYLEY: You didn't. We dragged you up that slope.

CHLOE: I knew I was drunk then. Last night wasn't the same.

HAYLEY: We're cold, knackered, hadn't eaten properly and hadn't drunk in nearly a week. It wouldn't take much.

CHLOE: But still.

HAYLEY: All I know is we were all loud, shouty, excitable and terrified. I don't know about you, but that sounds like me when I'm hammered.

CHLOE: You missed giggly, weepy and horny.

HAYLEY: Speak for yourself. It's all about the hangover horn for me.

CHLOE: That's the last thing I want. Give me fried food, leave me to nap all day and I'm sorted.

HAYLEY: Clears your head. Gives you something to do other than feeling shit.

CHLOE: Lisa didn't drink.

HAYLEY: I know. She doesn't.

CHLOE: But if she didn't drink this can't all be because of the shitty vodka. Why would she be acting as mental as the rest of us?

HAYLEY: Hysteria? An inbuilt desire to not stand out from a crowd? Because the fumes of that stuff alone are enough to make you trip balls? I don't know.

CHLOE: But you knew she didn't drink?

HAYLEY: Yep. Her dad was an alchy.

CHLOE: Shit.

HAYLEY: Drank himself to death when she was thirteen. Was the first funeral I'd ever gone to.

CHLOE: I've only ever been to one.

HAYLEY: Yeah.

CHLOE: I didn't know.

HAYLEY: Not the kind of thing you broadcast. So don't tell her I said anything. It's not exactly my secret to share.

CHLOE: It wasn't the vodka.

HAYLEY: Okay. It wasn't. What's the next theory?

CHLOE: That there's something out here.

HAYLEY: There is. Keith.

She gestures to the Snowman.

CHLOE: I'm serious.

HAYLEY: So am I.

CHLOE: You said you recognised the voice.

HAYLEY: I was drunk.

CHLOE: Who did you think it was?

HAYLEY: Doesn't matter.

CHLOE: It might.

HAYLEY: What do you want, for this to be some Scooby-Doo mystery for us all to solve?

CHLOE: I just want to know what the fuck is going on.

HAYLEY: What difference would it make? Either we were all drunk and scared ourselves shitless over nothing. Or, someone is fucking with us. And if someone is fucking with us there's not a thing we can do about it. We're half way up a fucking mountain. We've got two choices. That way to the top or back the way we came. That's it.

CHLOE: Whose voice do you think it was?

HAYLEY: And if it is someone fucking with us then they are definitely behind us cos there's no way they could have got ahead. So there's no choice. We go that way and beat them to the top. Show them they can't scare us off or fuck with our heads. We show them we don't give a flying fuck what they think, and carry on.

ZOE approaches.

ZOE: Things were getting a bit intimate in there. We might want to give them ten minutes.

CHLOE: You don't think it was the booze any more than I do.

HAYLEY: I want it to be the booze, Chloe. I really, really want it to be the booze. Because if it's not, and there is something on the mountain that's trying to fuck with us, then we're fucked. Wanna know why?

CHLOE: Why?

HAYLEY: Because last night we all told you to smash our only lifeline into tiny little pieces.

INSIDE THE TENT

LISA: It must be nice to believe in something. To 'have faith'.

RACHEL: Only atheists say that. Everyone else knows better.

LISA: I'd like to think there was something bigger out there. Something more than just this.

RACHEL: I wish there wasn't. I would love it if tomorrow they found proof it was all a lie.

LISA: You're like an inverse Fox Mulder. 'I don't want to believe'.

RACHEL: Okay. Stop me when you hear anything beneficial; from birth to grave you spend your life being told you're an imperfect failure, all thanks to a fuckwit called Adam who ignored one simple instruction, and took some fruit from the only tree in the entire world he was told not to touch.

LISA: Human nature. Tell a guy not to do something and it's the first thing he'll do just to see what happens. If God knows everything he should've known that one was coming!

RACHEL: Some dick from thousands of years ago eats a bit of fruit God told him not to and he curses every human who'll ever be born with sin. Every single one of us. We're all automatically sinners cos one man couldn't keep his fucking hands to himself.

LISA: And you actually believe that? Adam and Eve, the snake, the garden. All of it?

RACHEL: I don't want to. It's the most bullshit sounding story in the world. A picture book version of how life started. A pretty garden with one man, one woman, lots of trees and a naughty snake.

LISA: A very naughty snake. Love it. I hope that's how it's actually written.

RACHEL: There's only one rule and everyone is happy. Just don't touch God's tree.

LISA: It's where he stashes his porn.

RACHEL: But one day a naughty snake comes and tells the woman that the fruit on God's tree is the best. And the woman tells the man. Which gets the man thinking.

LISA: Hang on. Why does the snake tell Eve first?

RACHEL: So that from that point on women can be blamed for everything. These were two guys cocking about, but because it went via someone with tits it was really all her fault.

LISA: You don't sound like you're a fan of this story.

RACHEL: I'm not. I hate it. It's fucking stupid, anyone can see that. But I've also spent a lifetime of being told it's the truth. God's truth. I want to say fuck it. But what if I'm wrong?

LISA: Deathbed conversion? That's always been my plan if I suddenly see a white light.

RACHEL: I fucking wish. We don't get offered that. When you die, you die. Gone. Done. Until one day, after God's stopped pissing about and finally told Satan to fuck off, he's going to resurrect us. All of us.

LISA: Everyone?

RACHEL: Everyone. Well. Nearly everyone. Some burn in Gehenna but they don't tell you who, so there's wiggle room.

LISA: But if everyone's coming back what's to worry about?

RACHEL: Because we get resurrected for one reason. To be judged. That's the only reason why any of us are here the first time round. As a test. A chance for God to see if we're suitable for his super swanky VIP paradise he's got in the works.

LISA: God sounds like a wanker.

RACHEL: He is! He really fucking is! The God I was taught isn't a god of love, or forgiveness. He's a childish dick who wants everyone to worship him in the way he decrees. Just believing in him isn't enough. You have to spend an entire life jumping through hoops to see if you qualify for round two. Worshipping him and thanking him for the privilege of being allowed to live. And if you haven't impressed him, or grovelled hard enough, you're fucked.

LISA: And so this is you just getting the fucking in early?

RACHEL: No. This is me being too shit scared to make a decision either way.

LISA: You seem pretty clear about it to me. The swearing. The sex. Doesn't exactly scream devout disciple.

RACHEL: That's the point. It was my big fuck you to my parents and to God. Look at me. I'm my own person. You're telling me I'm imperfect well look how fucking imperfect I can be.

LISA: Seems pretty successful to me.

RACHEL: So why do I still pray for forgiveness every single fucking night? Pray to a god I hate to forgive me for trying to live a life without the bastard in it?

LISA: You're a complex soul, Rach.

RACHEL: Don't even get me started on the fucking soul stuff.

LISA: But if it's not making your life better then why do it at all? Why not just stop?

RACHEL: Well, that's the question, isn't it? Picture it this way: If you decided one day that oxygen was a lie, you'd try not to breathe. Maybe lots of other people have told you they don't breathe and so you want to try it too. So you hold your breath for as long as you can. You'd go blue in the face and hurt from the strain. Your body fights it but you force it. You try to hold back. But sooner or later you're going to take another breath…

HAYLEY, **ZOE** *and* **CHLOE** *return.*

ZOE: Not interrupting, are we?

LISA: Rachel's just been taking witness.

HAYLEY: Christ. Have you seen the light?

RACHEL: Cliff notes version; God's a cunt.

LISA: I'm going to do a bit of shopping around. Maybe try the Mormons first.

55

CHLOE: They all have lovely teeth.

HAYLEY: Not a chance. Think of all the shirts you'd have to iron.

LISA: It's decision time.

HAYLEY: No fair. I haven't checked out Buddha yet.

LISA: Today's our eleventh day of trekking, so according to our schedule we really should reach the peak today.

ZOE: Sounds good to me.

LISA: But we can't ignore the fact we don't have any way to contact the outside world anymore. If anything goes wrong, we're screwed.

ZOE: We've come this far.

LISA: Since, for one reason or another, we didn't manage to signal last night, chances are someone's going to be coming looking for us fairly soon. And they'll be coming to our last known location. Right here.

HAYLEY: So we either stay put and freeze our arses off, or head out and actually do what we intended to do? Easy decision.

LISA: There is a third option.

RACHEL: The orgy. My time to shine.

LISA: We head back.

HAYLEY: No fucking way.

LISA: Hear me out.

HAYLEY: No. It's not an option.

LISA: It's not a nice one, but we have to consider every possibility.

HAYLEY: No. I won't. If you go back then you're going without me.

ZOE: And me.

CHLOE: No one is going anywhere without anyone. Whatever we do we're doing together.

RACHEL: If you try to unite us in song now I will literally end you.

LISA: I was thinking maybe we should vote. Seems the fairest way.

HAYLEY: Sure. Vote if you want but it won't make any difference. I am not going back down this mountain.

LISA: I'm saying we should hear what everyone thinks, that's all.

HAYLEY: Good. Everyone is entitled to their own opinion. You want to fuck off home, I'm happy for you. But I'm staying.

LISA: Hayley, that's not fair.

HAYLEY: Life's not fucking fair.

LISA: If it were we wouldn't have accidentally broken the radio putting us in this shitty position.

HAYLEY: This has nothing to do with the radio being broken and you know it.

LISA: What do you mean?

HAYLEY: Chloe was right. We weren't drunk last night and we weren't imagining it. There's someone out there and you know as well as I do who it is.

LISA: Eleven days in and someone final snaps.

HAYLEY: That was Paul's voice. He's fucking with us all just to fuck with me.

CHLOE: Hayley…

HAYLEY: You heard it too. You know I'm right. He's probably camped half a mile that way broadcasting his stupid numbers thinking we'll run home. Run right past him so he can see how much of a failure I am.

RACHEL: Did it sound like Paul?

CHLOE: I didn't think so.

LISA: Last night was shit, and I can't pretend to know what was going on but if we all just stay calm and rational we'll sort this out.

HAYLEY: Calm and rational? My fucked up ex is hiding somewhere on the mountain to screw with us. Calm and rational can fuck off.

RACHEL: Okay. If he's up here then let's go find him. If he wants to be a weird creepy fucker then we'll go and show him what he's up against.

CHLOE: I really don't think it was him.

HAYLEY: Of course it was! What the fuck was it if it wasn't?

This hangs for a long time. Nobody has an answer.

LISA: Either way I think we agree we're not just staying here. Let's start packing up and we'll see how we feel.

They start to pack away all the equipment. Nobody speaks.

CHLOE: Has anyone ever died in one of their dreams?

HAYLEY: Nice one Chlo. Keep it light.

LISA: I don't think you can. Don't you die in real life if you die in a dream?

CHLOE: That's a myth. You usually just wake up.

RACHEL: I hardly ever remember my dreams.

LISA: I try not to. The more you try the quicker it vanishes.

HAYLEY: I used to keep the Dreamer's Guide book by my bed to help understand what it all meant.

CHLOE: And did it?

HAYLEY: No. It's all bollocks. The subconscious isn't supposed to make sense.

RACHEL: Mine never does.

HAYLEY: Nobody's does. Trying to make sense of dreams is just pissing in the wind.

RACHEL: I must be an expert then!

ZOE: You can add meaning to anything if you try. I was running last night. You could say I was running toward something or away from something. That it's a sign of moving forward and change, or that I'm running from change. You can spin in however you want.

LISA: Falling asleep in dreams is weird too.

CHLOE: Dreams within dreams?

RACHEL: Fuck we've already covered *Lost*, let's not do *Inception* too.

CHLOE: I hate days where it feels like you have to wake up three or four times when you've actually only been woken in a dream. It's exhausting.

HAYLEY: Better than the old turning up to school naked one.

LISA: Oh, I HATE that feeling!

HAYLEY: Awake I know it's stupid dream logic, but at the time I always have the same thought – how have I not noticed I'm naked until I'm actually here?

CHLOE: And it's only when you notice that suddenly everyone else notices too.

RACHEL: Then it's 'Shit! Do I cover up and run or style this out?'

LISA: How do you style out suddenly being naked?

RACHEL: Easy. You just make everyone else get naked too.

CHLOE: Like in a lucid dream.

RACHEL: One where you know you're dreaming?

CHLOE: Where you know you're dreaming and can control things?

RACHEL: I wish. When I know I'm dreaming I wake up. My subconscious creates the nudity all on it's own. Thanks brain.

ZOE: It's a shit feeling being trapped in a dream.

HAYLEY: So who was running naked through your mind last night?

RACHEL: Wouldn't you like to know?

CHLOE: I dreamt of the numbers.

Someone's said it. Everyone did. Everyone's freaked, but tries to brush it off.

HAYLEY: That's weird. Me too.

LISA: And me.

ZOE: Same here.

HAYLEY: Not even with any context. Just the numbers over and over.

ZOE: Like a blizzard.

CHLOE: 19. 14. 15. 23…

RACHEL: Is this fucking with anyone else or is it just me?

LISA: We had a scare and we were all jumpy. We've been in each other's pockets for nearly two weeks, seeing the same things and talking about the same crap. It's no surprise we've ended up dreaming about the same shit too.

CHLOE: But not like that?

LISA: Like Hayley said you can throw any meaning you like at it and something will stick. It's coincidence.

RACHEL: It was really fucked up.

LISA: We're not going to talk about it. We're all going to go for a piss, then we're going to pack the tent and we're going to climb to the top of this mountain.

HAYLEY: What happened to voting?

LISA: Fuck voting. I'm game if you are.

HAYLEY: If you're asking that's literally the same thing.

LISA: To the top of the hill.

RACHEL: We're not doing some three musketeers shit, if that's what that was supposed to be.

LISA: Fine. Be miserable. But first, a piss.

HAYLEY: This is the longest after waking up I've gone without.

RACHEL: Stand aside, ladies. You're about to witness something special.

LISA: You can just wait. We've bagsied the Shewees.

RACHEL: Fuck that. Today's a momentous day. I'm writing my name in the snow!

She exits.

HAYLEY: Won't be long.

ZOE: It's fine, we'll just finish off.

CHLOE: Bladder of iron, me.

    LISA *and* **HAYLEY** *exit.*

ZOE: Iron would rust. You mean you've got a bladder of steel.

CHLOE: If you say so.

ZOE: What's up?

CHLOE: Nothing.

ZOE: Lies.

CHLOE: I think I'm just ready for home.

ZOE: Then I've got some bad news for you. It's taken you eleven days to get here and there's no ski lift or magic slide back down. Even if we reach the peak today, that's still eleven days before we're home.

CHLOE: I know.

ZOE: It's been fun though.

CHLOE: Yeah.

ZOE: Hasn't it?

CHLOE: I said yeah.

ZOE: Didn't sound like you meant it.

CHLOE: I'm just tired.

ZOE: Climbing and trekking. It's hard work.

CHLOE: You make it look easy.

ZOE: I'm built for it.

CHLOE: That's not what I meant.

ZOE: I've always walked lots. Found hills to scramble. Disappeared on my own to 'be one with nature'.

CHLOE: The exercise is the easy bit.

ZOE: Quality alone time. Chance to clear your head.

CHLOE: It's the nights. The chat. The constant shite.

ZOE: Sod off, that's where you shine!

CHLOE: It's hard work. And if I stop or I let it drop it's suddenly all 'ooh what's wrong? What's got you down? You depressed? Happy love? Tell your face.'

ZOE: We've all been there. 'Chin up, it might never happen!' You don't have to be upbeat all the time.

CHLOE: Apparently I do.

ZOE: Nobody expects you to be happy 24/7.

CHLOE: Of course they do. That's why they like me. I'm the fun one. The cute one. The silly one. The adorable, sweet smushable one.

ZOE: Nothing wrong with that.

CHLOE: And I'm everyone's friend. Chloe's your shoulder to cry on. Chloe will help you out. Chloe will cheer you up.

ZOE: Who wouldn't want to be that guy?

CHLOE: It's great. Love it. Go me. Until one of those friends kills herself and basically blames you for not being there.

ZOE: That escalated quickly.

CHLOE: 'I messaged Chloe.' That's what she wrote. 'I messaged Chloe and she didn't read it. Too busy for me.' How else would you read into it?

ZOE: I'd forgotten about that.

CHLOE: Ten minutes later, she's swallowed a box of pills and cut open her wrists. Doesn't take a psychic to know that if I'd answered the message there might just have been something I could have done.

ZOE: Chloe.

CHLOE: The stupid thing is I wasn't even doing anything. Sat on Tinder swiping left on dick pics. I literally had my phone in my hand. It would've taken a second to send back a 'Hey'. But you know what? I couldn't be bothered.

ZOE: You couldn't have known, you can't blame yourself.

CHLOE: Why not? She did.

ZOE: Of course she didn't. You were her friend. Probably her best friend.

CHLOE: I hardly knew her! I was nice to her because I'm nice to everyone. Christ, I probably had more conversations with the server in the canteen than I ever did with her.

ZOE: That's ridiculous.

CHLOE: Is it?

ZOE: You were inseparable at Dean's birthday.

CHLOE: She latched onto me! I was the only one she was talking to, so I did the nice thing and stayed with her.

ZOE: Because you're a good friend.

CHLOE: Because I'm a nice person. That's all. I go through the motions because that's what you do. Met up with her a few times. Brought her along to a few things to introduce her to people. Is that actually kindness?

ZOE: Obviously!

CHLOE: Is it though? Or was it so she might pick up some new people and be less of a burden to me? Christ if I'd known just how much she was relying on me I'd have actually put some effort in!

ZOE: Nobody knew. You can't predict these things.

CHLOE: After it happened, her parents wanted to talk to me. I thought they were going to blame me. They should've done, they had every right to.

ZOE: Don't talk like that.

CHLOE: But do you know what they did? Thanked me. Thanked me for being such a good friend to their daughter when she'd been struggling. I've never felt like more of a fraud.

ZOE: I didn't know any of this.

CHLOE: They gave me her journal. Thought I'd find it comforting. Said it didn't feel right for them to know 'those' thoughts of hers, they're what she should be sharing with friends. So they gave it to me. Her 'best friend'.

ZOE: They weren't to know.

CHLOE: l feel guilty every time I look at it. Sick to the stomach guilt. I thought about throwing it away but that would've been even worse.

ZOE: She can't have meant for any of this to happen.

CHLOE: So when this expedition was arranged, this trek in her honour, I knew what I could do with it.

She unzips her rucksack and pulls out a journal.

CHLOE: Do the decent thing and lay her to rest.

OUTSIDE THE TENT

HAYLEY *and* **LISA** *are packing up the outside equipment.*

HAYLEY: What's the plan if we actually make it?

LISA: What do you mean?

HAYLEY: I'll be honest, I've never thought this far ahead. When we actually reach the top what do we do? Take a selfie, down some Albanian turpentine then swivel and head right back down again?

LISA: Pretty much.

HAYLEY: Should one of us say something, do you think?

LISA: By 'one of us', you mean me.

HAYLEY: You're the best candidate. Rachel's would be too blasphemous; mine would sound insincere; I don't think Chloe's in a good enough place right now and –

LISA: I hardly knew her!

HAYLEY: It doesn't have to be detailed. 'This was for you… Blah, blah, we miss you'. Done.

LISA: Then you do it!

HAYLEY: I can't. Wouldn't be right.

LISA: Why?

HAYLEY: I'm not even sure I liked her!

LISA: 'This was for you… Blah, blah. Some people kinda miss you. Not me. But y'know. Can't please everyone.' Done! Perfect.

HAYLEY: Very moving. I only hope such kind words are said about me one day.

RACHEL approaches. From the way she's walking it appears she's wet herself.

RACHEL: Well, that was a fucking mess!

HAYLEY: What went wrong? Forget how to spell your name?

RACHEL: Oi, who's been fucking about with Aled?

She moves to the snowman. Some of his features have been altered.

LISA: I thought we'd called him Keith?

RACHEL: Been changing his name as well as his outfit?

LISA: He's always been called Keith.

HAYLEY: And we haven't touched him since we made him.

RACHEL: Yeah, yeah.

HAYLEY: Seriously we haven't.

RACHEL: Let's fuck about with Rachel some more, she can take it.

LISA: She's lost it.

RACHEL: Did you think I wouldn't notice?

HAYLEY: Notice what?

RACHEL: Where are they then? What stupid place am I going to find them turning up next?

HAYLEY: Rachel, what the fuck are you talking about it.

RACHEL: My knickers. The ones I'd hilariously shoved in Aled-Keith's pocket yesterday after I complimented him on having such massive snowballs.

LISA: We haven't touched them.

RACHEL: Yeah, hilarious. I'm sure they'll magically appear in the kettle or something sometime soon. Hope you've given Chloe her gloves back though, she only brought two pairs.

LISA spots hers are now on the Snowman.

LISA: Who switched them for mine? These were at the bottom of my bag. Who the fuck has been going through my stuff?

HAYLEY: If this is a funny full points for commitment but it can stop now.

RACHEL breaks off a piece of the snowman's head. Inside the snowball is a bra.

RACHEL: That's mine! When the fuck did someone have time to hide that in there?

LISA: When we were making it. Someone's been fucking with all of us from the start.

Inside the tent **CHLOE** *screams.*

HAYLEY: What the fuck?

They rush back inside.

INSIDE THE TENT

CHLOE *is cowering in a corner with* **ZOE** *trying to offer her support. She's thrown the journal across the room.*

ZOE: It's okay, I've got this.

LISA: What happened?

CHLOE: I'd forgotten… It was so mental last night I didn't realise.

HAYLEY: Realise what?

CHLOE: Snowmen exist.

ZOE: Don't be silly.

RACHEL: What the fuck are you talking about.

CHLOE: Snowmen exist!

LISA: The message in numbers?

CHLOE: That's what she wrote. In her journal. It's the last thing she wrote.

RACHEL: You're taking the piss. You're all taking the piss.

CHLOE: Read it!

LISA picks up the journal and finds the last entry. She reads out loud:

LISA: 'I read back through my old journals. Found some cringy school poetry. What was I even thinking? One stood out. I don't even remember writing it but it keeps going round and round my head. "A Snowman is a frozen reflection, Of a purer life we all have missed, An ice cold shell built with your friends, We know now snowmen exist."'

Nobody knows what to say. Is this even happening? The wind outside is back but now sounds like the static of the numbers.

ZOE: Okay. This is all seriously fucked up and Christ knows I'm probably the last person who should be trying to pull us all together. I never know what to say and I'm seriously struggling right now. But if we forget everything and concentrate on just getting to the top. Nothing else. We scale the Yapstovals and we deal with the rest of whatever this is when we're done.

CHLOE: For fuck's sake Zoe, will you just shut the fuck up!

And everyone freezes, looking at **CHLOE**.

RACHEL: Are you okay?

CHLOE: I'm so sick of you going on and on.

HAYLEY: Who?

CHLOE: Zoe!

ZOE: I'm sorry.

CHLOE: No. I'm sorry, I shouldn't have snapped. This is all too much.

LISA: Chloe. Are you talking to Zoe?

CHLOE: Okay, sorry *everyone.*

HAYLEY: Is this actually happening?

LISA: Have you been talking to Zoe this whole time?

CHLOE: Someone's got to. You lot don't seem to make much of an effort.

RACHEL: Chloe… Zoe's why we're here.

CHLOE: Yeah. *(To* **ZOE**.*)* You were the one who suggested we should do this. It's your fault we're up this sodding mountain.

HAYLEY: This is so fucked. Are you even serious?

ZOE: I'm sorry Chloe. This is my fault. But you're wrong with what you said before. I didn't blame you.

LISA: Zoe's dead.

HAYLEY: That's her journal.

RACHEL: She killed herself three months ago.

An awful, awful silence. The play now switches perspective and we see events without **ZOE**. **CHLOE** *still reacts as though she's present.* **ZOE** *steps out and begins to very* *slowly disassemble the snowman outside. (**ZOE** no longer speaks but her dialogue from **CHLOE**'s perspective is included in brackets for clarity.)*

CHLOE: That's sick.

LISA: Chloe…

CHLOE: No, that's a really shitty thing to say. Too far. Way too far.

RACHEL: You're taking the piss, aren't you?

CHLOE: I know this is just a big joke to you but I'm actually trying to make this thing mean something.

HAYLEY: Can we just calm the fuck down for a second so I can actually process this…

*(**ZOE**: I'm sorry, Chloe…)*

CHLOE: For Christ's sake will you stop apologising and stand up for yourself for once? Why am I fighting your battles for you? Speak to them!

RACHEL: She's lost it. Eleven days in and someone finally snaps.

CHLOE: Zoe, this isn't my fight. Tell them!

LISA: Chloe, if Zoe's here with us then why are we here? What made us decide to climb the Yapstovals?

CHLOE: I'm not doing this anymore. Ask her yourself.

RACHEL: This is so fucked.

LISA: Chloe…

CHLOE: No. I'm done. I don't know what game you're playing, and I don't care anymore…

HAYLEY: Game? You think this is a game?

CHLOE: Some shitty psychological freak out to stop me from feeling guilty.

RACHEL: We're freaking you out?

CHLOE: Well done. Mission complete. I'm over it.

LISA: I think we all just need to take a minute…

CHLOE: You all want to pretend Zoe's my imaginary friend, you fill your boots. *(To Zoe.)* And you want to let them? Go for it. Congratulations. It's the most interesting thing you've done all trip.

RACHEL: What the fuck do we do now?

HAYLEY: Paul put you up to this, didn't he?

> **CHLOE** *doesn't react. From her perspective,* **HAYLEY** *asked this question to Zoe.*

LISA: We need to get off this mountain. Forget scaling the summit, we need to get home, quickly as we can.

HAYLEY: Giving me the silent treatment now I've figured it out?

> *(***ZOE:*** *I don't know what to say.)*

CHLOE: *(To Zoe.)* Did he? Is that why you're doing this?

HAYLEY: I'm not going to take your shit anymore. Tell me the truth or so help me I'll fucking leave you both up here to rot.

RACHEL: Back the fuck off. I'm not gonna pretend I know what's going on but talking like that isn't gonna fix it.

CHLOE: Don't start standing up for her, that's what she wants. It's a cry for attention.

HAYLEY: So you admit it?

CHLOE: Admit what?

HAYLEY: He talked you into fucking with us. All the weird shit. It's been you.

LISA: Can we not do this now?

RACHEL: Hayley, shut up. She hasn't turned into a fucking psycho.

HAYLEY: No. She hasn't. She's always been one.

CHLOE: You're right. She has.

HAYLEY: Not her, Chloe. You. You and my fucked up creep of an ex.

CHLOE: Me? *(Indicating Zoe.)* She's the one who's done this!

RACHEL: Chloe, there's no one there…

CHLOE grabs RACHEL's hand and rubs it over the absent 'Zoe's' face.

CHLOE: You sure about that? Can you feel her now, or am I making it up? Feels pretty real to me. Maybe slap her if you want to be really sure, I know I want to.

RACHEL: Chloe, you're frightening me now. Stop it. Please.

CHLOE: Or would you prefer to feel down here, would that convince you?

She moves her hand lower on 'Zoe'. RACHEL instinctively pulls away. LISA steps into the space where 'Zoe' has been stood.

LISA: If Zoe's alive, who killed themself? Who are we climbing this mountain for?

HAYLEY: Don't waste your time.

CHLOE: What?

HAYLEY: The numbers, breaking the radio, hiding our clothes in the snowman, it was all you.

CHLOE: I haven't hidden anyone's clothes.

LISA: Who died, Chloe?

CHLOE: She was our friend. We should've been there for her. All of us.

LISA: Yes we should. For Zoe.

CHLOE's world collapses as the realisation hits her. The static outside gets louder. CHLOE's twitch is back. She no longer sees Zoe.

CHLOE: No…

HAYLEY: Fuck's sake, you can quit the act now.

During this, RACHEL has hunted out her Bible and started reciting the Lord's Prayer.

RACHEL: 'Our Father in the heavens, let your name be sanctified. Let your Kingdom come. Let your will take place, as in heaven, also on Earth. Give us today our bread for this day; and forgive us our debts, as we also have forgiven our debtors. And do not bring us into temptation but deliver us from the wicked one…"

LISA: Do you have to do that right now?

CHLOE: I just needed her to understand.

RACHEL: …We ask this in your son Jesus' name, amen.'

And in the static they hear the beeps. The cycle of numbers is playing from somewhere.

HAYLEY: What the fuck was that?

LISA: The radio! It has to be the radio…

She starts searching on the floor for the radio pieces.

HAYLEY: We smashed it?

CHLOE: I broke it. She told me to break it!

LISA: Maybe it's not as fucked as we thought?

> **HAYLEY** *starts searching for the pieces.* **RACHEL** *looks to her Bible and then looks skyward in thanks. She mouths 'thank you'. But the numbers are getting louder. And now everyone is twitching again.*

LISA: Where the fuck is it?

RACHEL: Isn't this a piece?

CHLOE: It's not coming from in here. It's outside.

LISA: It can't be.

CHLOE: *(Shouting outside.)* Zoe? Zoe, is that you?

HAYLEY: It's him. If it's outside then it's got to be him, what else could it be?

RACHEL: 'Our Father in the heavens, let your name be sanctified. Let your Kingdom come…'

LISA: There is nothing out there. Okay? It's the radio. It has to be the radio…

RACHEL: … Let your will take place, as in heaven, also on Earth. Give us today our bread for this day; and forgive us our debts…

HAYLEY: *(Shouting outside.)* Stop hiding outside in the snow, you bastard. I'm not doing this anymore.

CHLOE: *(Shouting outside.)* I'm sorry, Zoe. I'm so, so sorry. I know it's my fault…

RACHEL: … as we also have forgiven our debtors. And do not bring us into temptation but deliver us from the wicked one…'

LISA finds a piece of the radio. It's clearly lifeless. The static is impossibly loud, almost drowning them out.

LISA: No. No, that's impossible.

HAYLEY: *(Shouting outside.)* I'll never, ever, take you back. You're dead to me.

RACHEL: '…We ask this is Jesus' name…'

CHLOE: Zoe, I'm sorry. You're dead.

LISA: It's dead.

Blackout.

The numbers cycle plays once more all the way through then stops. The silence is deafening.

Then: BANG. An almighty crash/rumble – a landslide or avalanche, vast in proportion.

There is silence and darkness in the aftermath.

The lights return. The tent is a wreck. Bags have burst open. Equipment thrown everywhere. The girls' clothes are wet. Slowly, they look to each other, then outside the tent. The Snowman has completely disappeared, as has ZOE.

RACHEL: Aled's gone.

HAYLEY: You mean Keith.

LISA: Lost under the snow.

CHLOE: Poor guy.

LISA: We can't stay here.

HAYLEY: Yeah, I know.

CHLOE: Where else is there to go?

RACHEL: Out. We go out.

LISA: Finish what we started.

CHLOE: Can we still do that?

RACHEL: We can try.

HAYLEY: We're soaked. We'll freeze.

LISA: Then grab what you can.

They pick up what bits of clothing they can find. They're all mismatched.

CHLOE: …I'm sorry.

HAYLEY: No need. We're past that.

CHLOE: I know. But still…

RACHEL: We all are.

HAYLEY: So how are we going to do this? Just open up and run for it?

LISA: We can't use the door. I can't face Keith.

RACHEL: Aled.

LISA: Whatever his name was. I'd prefer to remember him as he was.

CHLOE: We can use this?

She pulls a knife from her backpack. For a moment no one is quite sure what she's suggesting.

CHLOE: Cut our way out. So there's no going back.

HAYLEY: Brutal.

LISA: Efficient.

RACHEL: I'm not even going to ask where you got that from.

CHLOE: The survival kit. I'm not a psycho.

RACHEL: Yeah, that's what they all say.

LISA: Are we sure about this?

HAYLEY: I'm game.

RACHEL: Me too. Are you?

LISA: I don't know.

CHLOE: We do this all together or not at all.

She holds up the knife against the edge of the tent.

RACHEL: All together.

She puts her hand on the knife.

HAYLEY *does the same.*

HAYLEY: …But I'm not saying the sentimental bullshit.

LISA *puts her hand on the knife.*

LISA: Together.

*ZOE enters from where the Snowman stood. She tears the final page out of her journal and hands it to **CHLOE**. She puts her hand on the knife.*

ZOE: All together.

And this time they can all see her.

They cut open the tent – the static returns – and one by one step out into the void.

POSTSCRIPT

Damn. I knew I'd forgotten something.

Page one, line one; add the following stage direction:

ZOE *isn't actually there.* <u>*Only*</u> **CHLOE** *can see and hear her. Nobody else reacts or interacts with her at all.*

And herein lies the challenge of staging *We Know Now Snowmen Exist*. In a group of just five, how do you portray three characters completely disregarding a fourth without the audience ever noticing?

The script jumps through all the necessary hoops to facilitate the rug pull; placing Zoe firmly as the socially awkward outsider, her dialogue in group discussions leaving little impact – her lines can be entirely removed from group discussions and the flow of conversation doesn't alter – and painstakingly engineering a few crucial moments of misdirection which appear to have her taking the lead. But these efforts are immaterial without being paired with confident performances, inventive staging and an almost obsessive eye for detail, to avoid the otherwise inevitable cry of 'Oh, well obviously I saw that coming…'

A few details to consider:

Zoe's possessions also aren't there. No one else can touch anything of hers, nor are they especially making space for her. Equally, she can't touch anything that isn't hers. Endeavour to avoid the audience proclaiming 'poltergeist' after the fact.

Eye contact is obviously a no-no. But it's vital to find a balance that works. There's often nothing more obvious that deliberately avoiding it.

Zoe's awkwardness helpfully gives her a tendency to speak during the off-beats of conversation. But don't forget that only Chloe is ever specifically leaving her the space to get a word in.

How aware Zoe is of her own limitations is deliberately left open to interpretation. As indeed is the answer to what Zoe actually is – a hallucination, a ghost, a memory, a trick, or something else entirely. There is, in my mind at least, a definitive solution. But the Dyatlov Pass buried its secrets. And sixty years of speculation sounds like a lot more fun.